Are We There Yet Grandma?

Felicity Newton
Illustrated by Jailyn Webb

To order additional copies of this book, contact:
Xlibris
1-800-455-039
www.xlibris.com.au
Orders@Xlibris.com.au

Illustrated by Jailyn Webb

ISBN: Softcover   978-1-7960-0530-1
       EBook   978-1-7960-0637-7

Print information available on the last page

Rev. date: 09/28/2019

Are We There Yet Grandma?

Felicity Newton

I would like to dedicate this book to my 3 beautiful grandchildren Tarj, Ivie, and Nylah.

Special thanks for the wonderful support of my husband Chris and my family.

I would also like to thank my very good friend Beth Hattenfels for believing in me.

Ivie wakes up early. She's excited to be going on a road trip with her grandma.

Mummy packs Ivie's bag and Ivie adds four of her favourite dolls; an iPad, four toy puppies and a book for the long five-hour car trip.

Ivie quickly gets dressed and eats her yummy, warm porridge. Then she brushes her teeth.

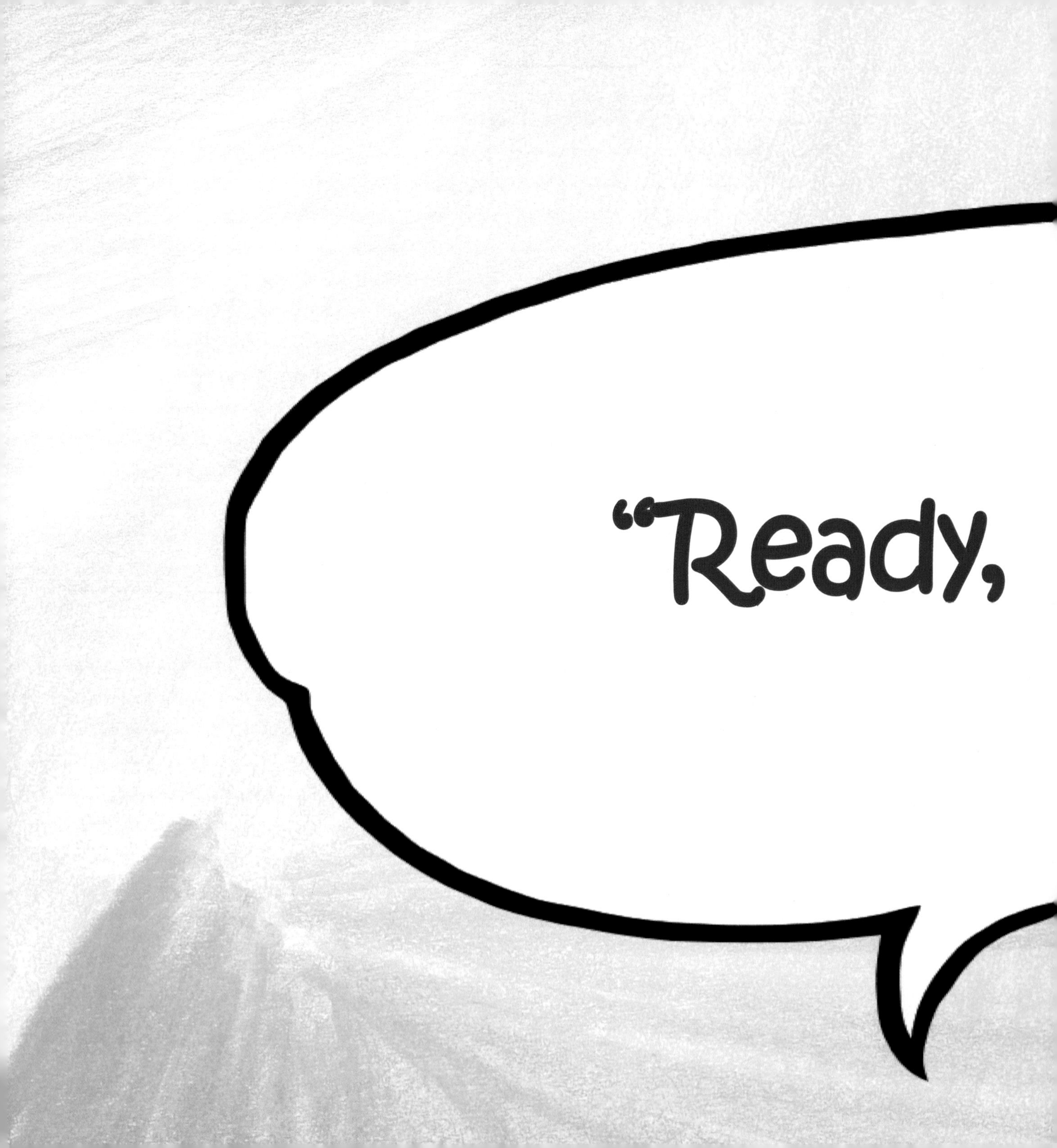
"Ready,

Ivie runs out to Grandma's little white car. When she gets there, she says goodbye to her big brother, Tarj; her baby sister Nylah and Indianna, their dachshund. Then she turns to her mummy and gives her a *biggggggg* cuddle and kiss before getting into the car.

Grandma makes sure that Ivie has her seat belt on and off they go.

Ivie yells out the window, "Bye, Mummy!"

Grandma pulls into the petrol station to fill her car up with fuel for the long trip home to the country. Grandma buys a packet of chicken chips for Ivie to eat for later on. Yummy!

Ivie looks out her window and sees lots of cars; caravans, roundabouts, buses, motorbikes and trucks *zooooooooming* past.

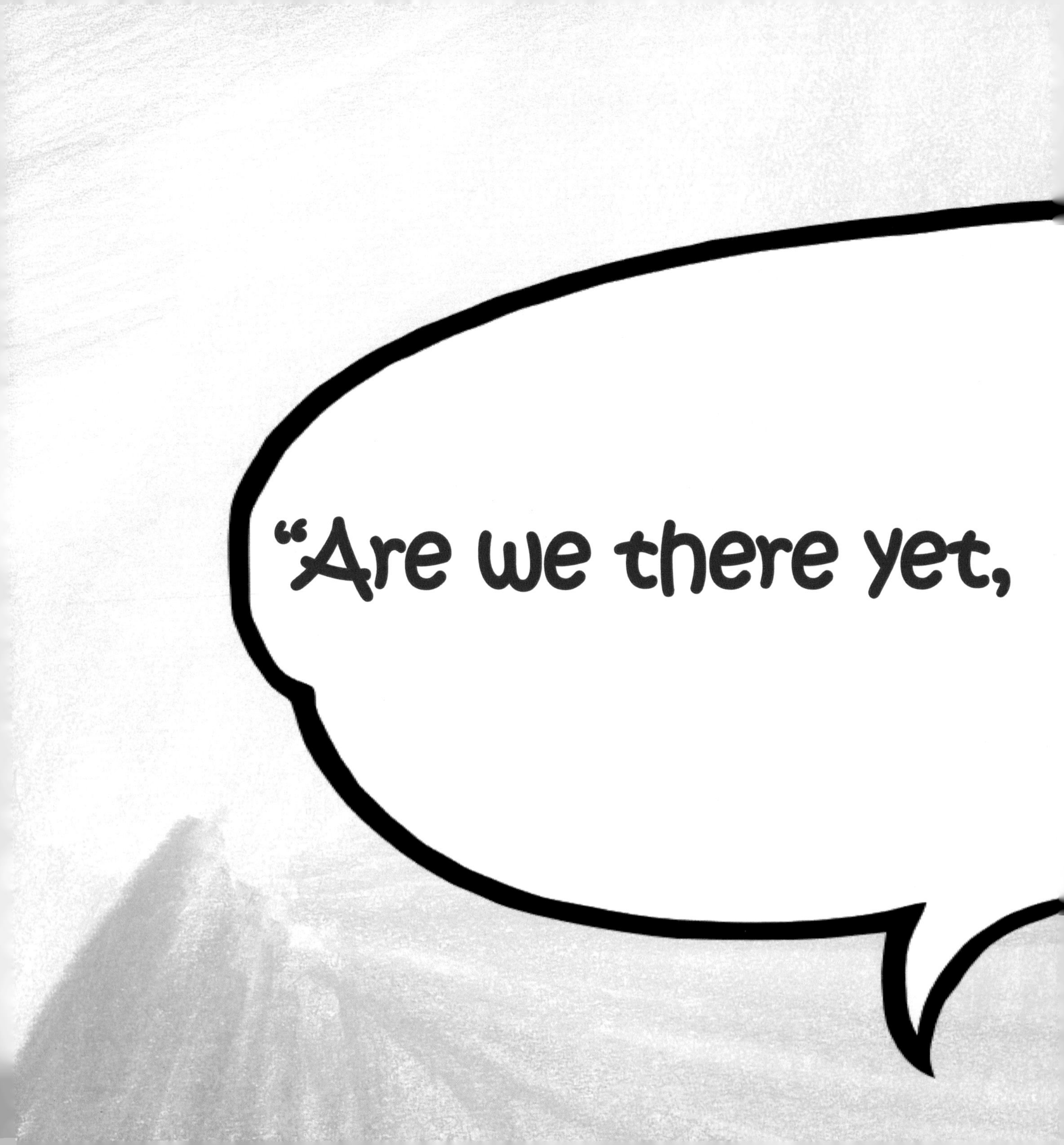
"Are we there yet,

"Not yet," says Grandma. "Look out your window and tell Grandma what else you can see."

Ivie looks out her window and sees big black clouds above. Then she sees a sunshower as the sun tries to peek through the clouds. Ivie hears the *pitter-patter, pitter-patter* of raindrops on the roof of Grandma's car.

Grandma turns on the windscreen wipers— *swwwwish swwwwish, swwwwish, swwwish*—to clear the rain off the windscreen.

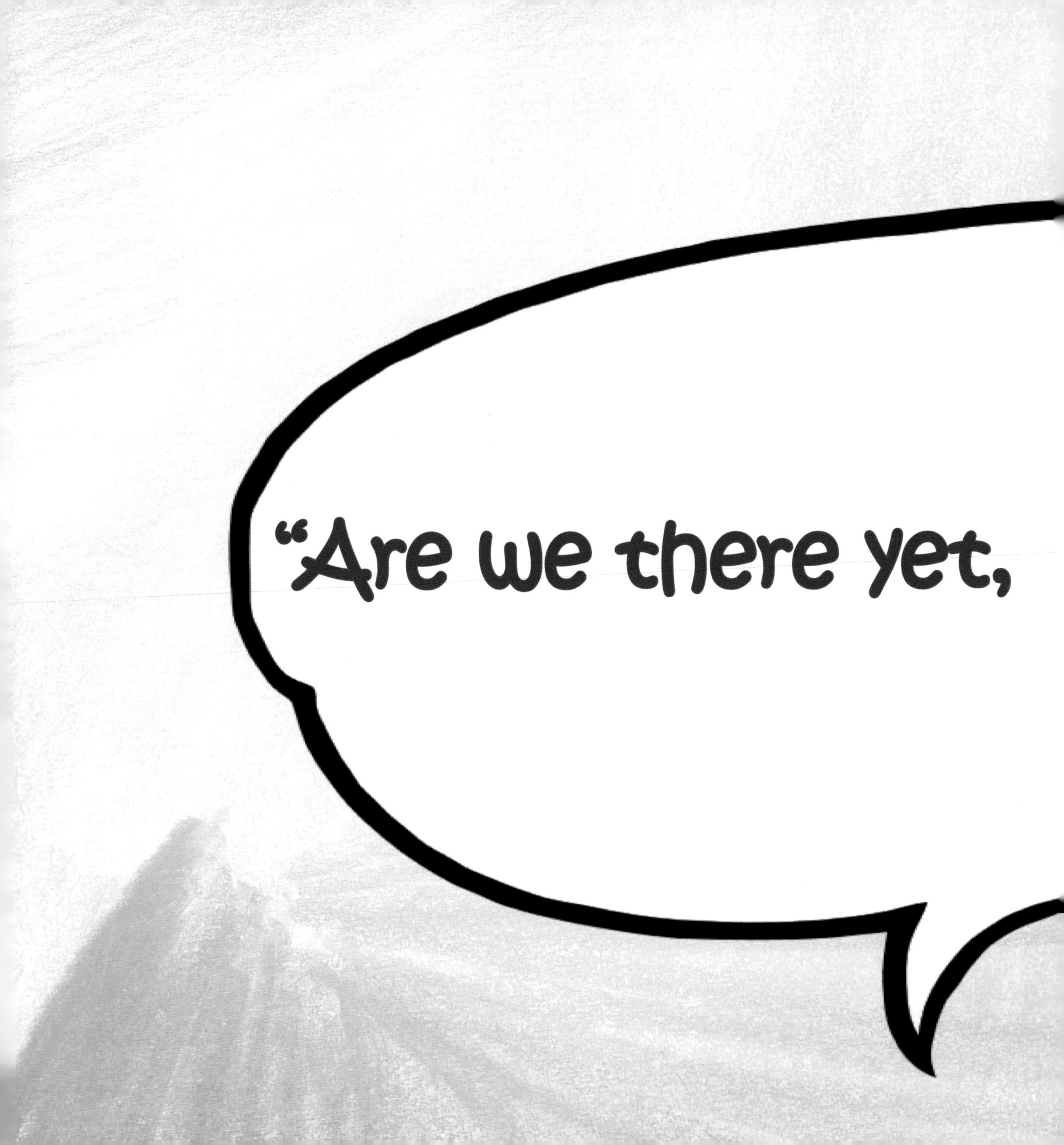
"Are we there yet,

"Not yet," says Grandma. "What else can you see out your window?"

Ivie looks out her window and sees lots of black-and-white cows, some white woolly sheep and horses with their pyjamas on.

Grandma points out the koala crossing that hangs across the busy freeway. It's for the little koalas to cross so that they can get to the other side safely. Ivie sees four koala crossings in total.

"Look, Grandma! Look at the big train as we drive over the bridge. The train goes underneath the bridge and has lots of carriages holding black coal."

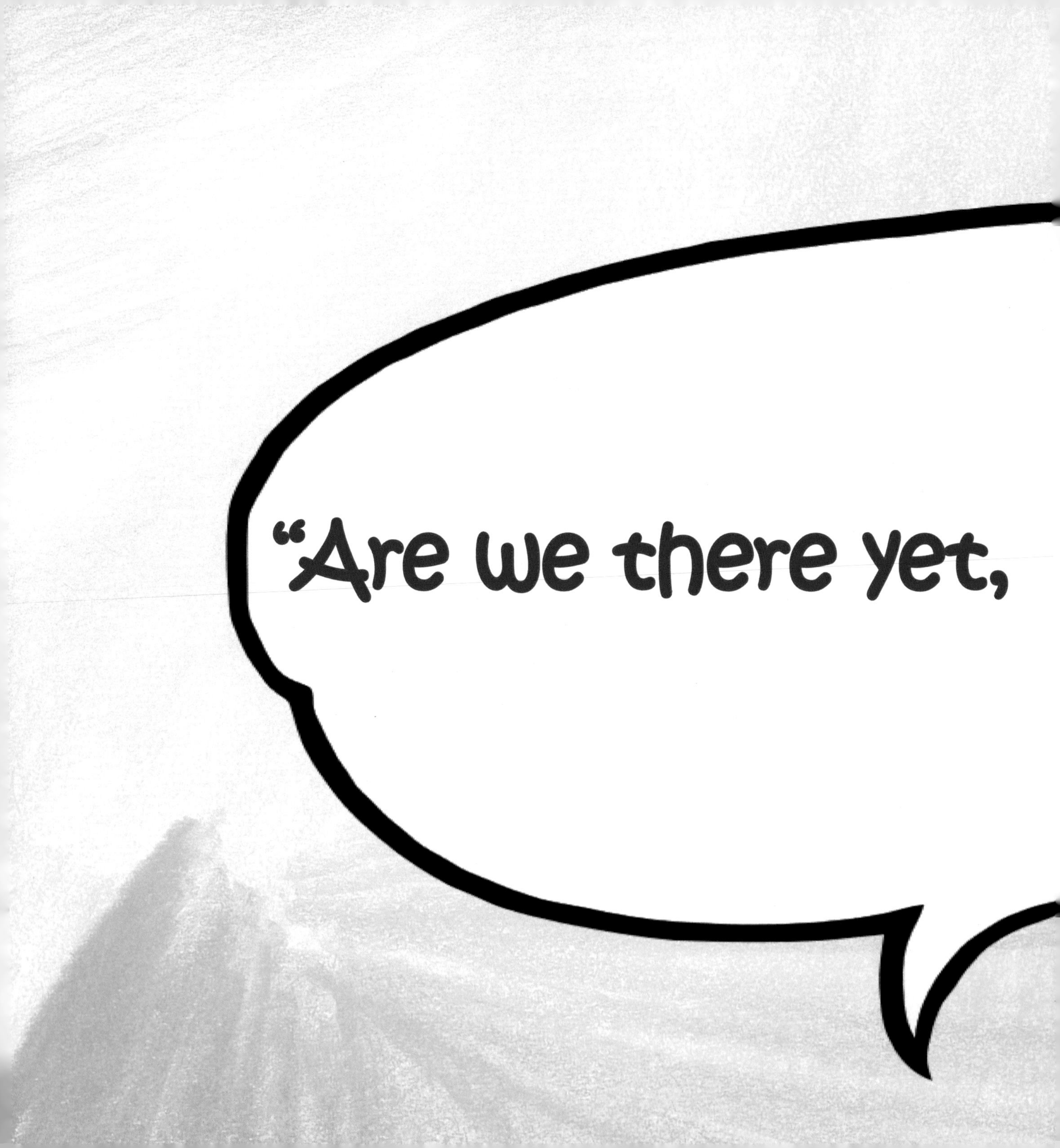
"Are we there yet,

"Not yet," says Grandma. "How about we sing some nursery rhymes, like 'Humpty Dumpty,' 'Hey Diddle Diddle,' 'Baa, Baa, Black Sheep,' 'Little Bo-Peep,' 'Incy Wincy Spider' and 'Hickory Dickory Dock'?"

"That's funny, Grandma. Can we sing them all again?"

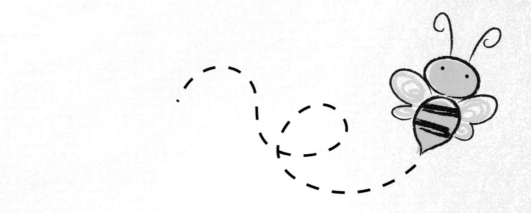

Grandma stops quickly at Horner's Honey Farm so she can drop off some large empty honey jars. Grandma also buys another big jar of their delicious sweet honey.

"The honey bees have been very busy making honey for you, Grandma," says Ivie.

"They sure have been," says Grandma with a smile.

Ivie can't wait to have honey and peanut butter toast for breakfast in the morning. Yummy!

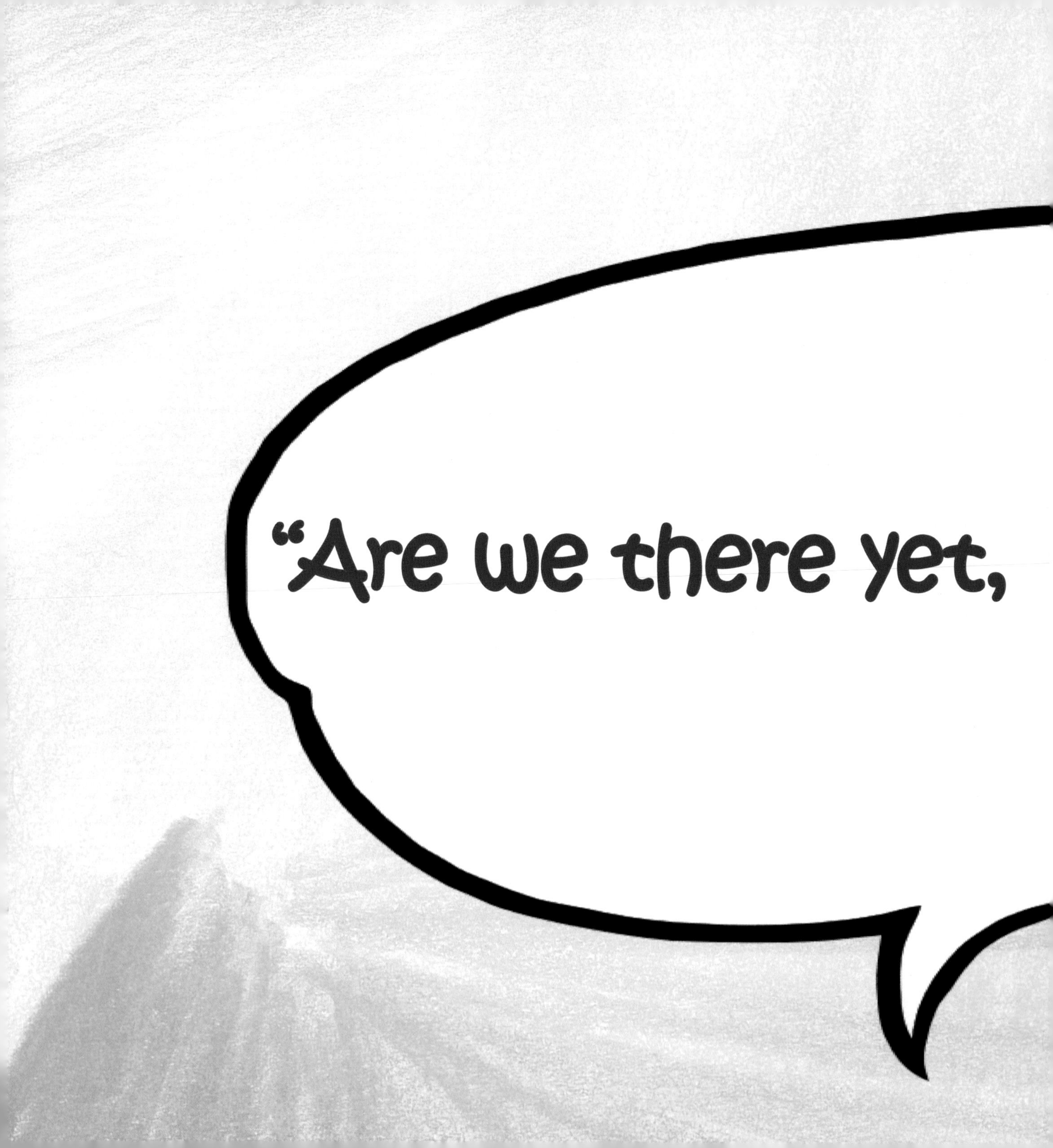
“Are we there yet,

"Not yet," says Grandma. "What else can you see out your window?"

Ivie looks out her window and sees some big mountains in the distance, lots of fluffy white clouds, birds flying up in the sky and a sleeping kangaroo on the side of the road!

They stop at a small town called Merriwa to have a short break and to stretch their legs. They go to a local café and Ivie has a babyccino and a piece of chocolate cake, while Grandma has a coffee and eats the remainder of Ivie's chocolate cake.

Ivie sees a lady walking some puppies on leads that remind her of their own puppy, Indianna the dachshund, who is back at home on the Central Coast.

When they are back in the car again, Ivie looks out her window and sees a big, beautiful, colourful rainbow up in the sky.

"Look, look, Grandma! Can you see the rainbow too?"

"Yes," says Grandma. "What colours can you see?"

Ivie looks up and says, "Pink, green, yellow, and orange."

"Gee, you're good with your colours," says Grandma.

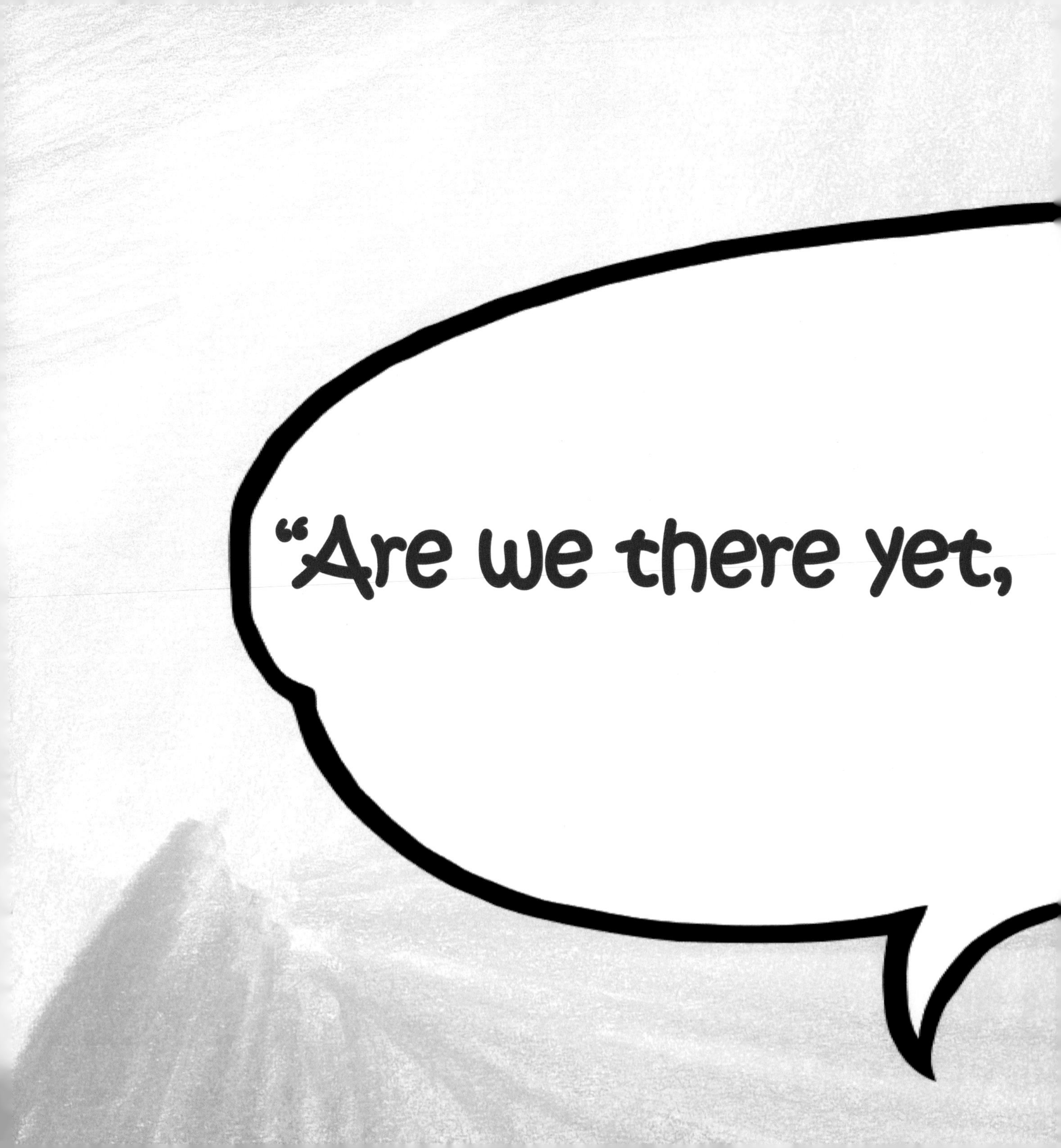
“Are we there yet,

"Not yet," says Grandma. "How about you close your eyes and have a sleep for a little while? When you wake up, we should nearly be home in Dubbo."

Ivie falls asleep and wakes up just before coming in to Dubbo.

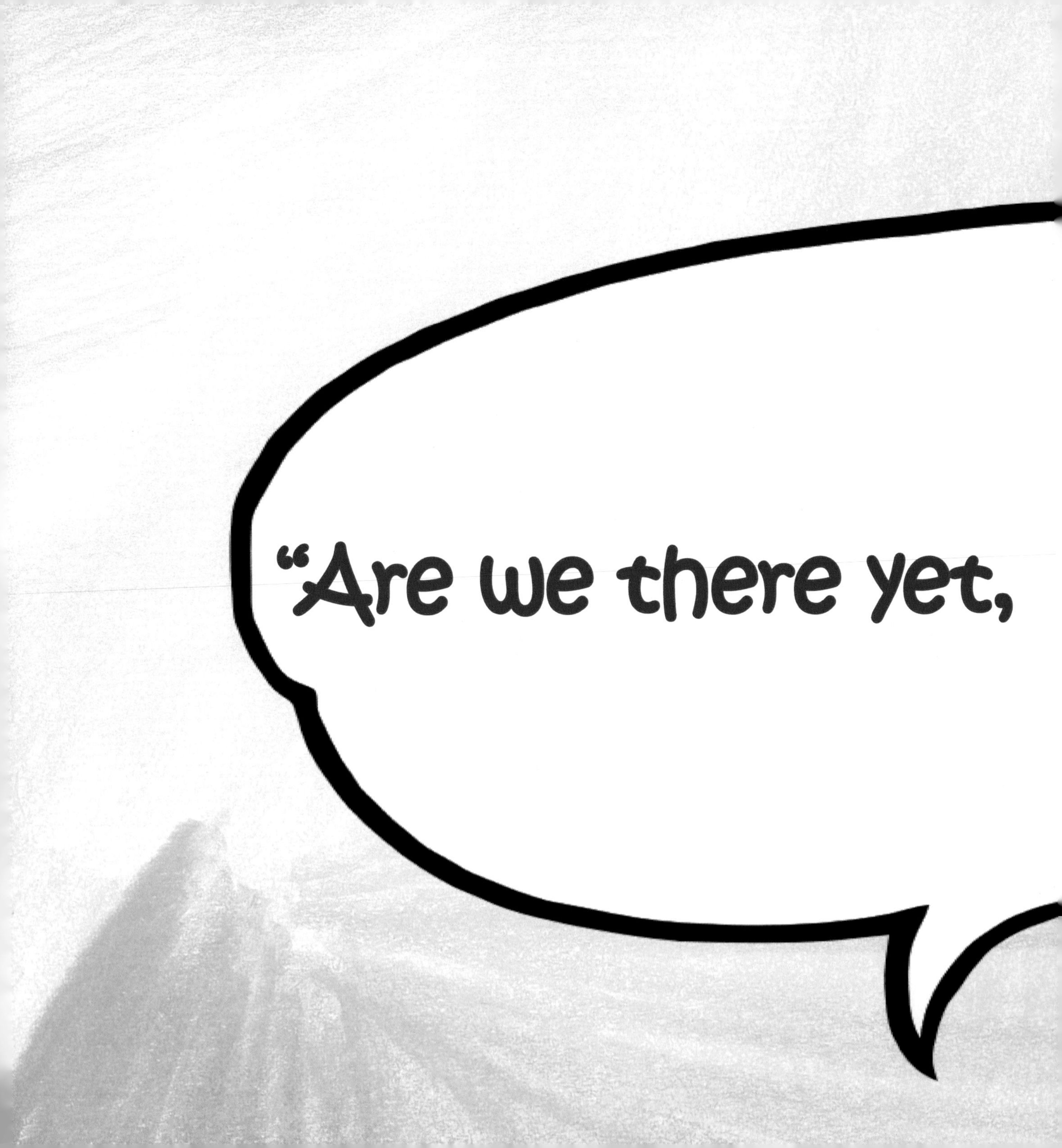
"Are we there yet,

"Yes," says Grandma.

"Yay!" says Ivie. They drive into Dubbo and Ivie sees some trees along the road side without leaves. "Why are there no leaves on the trees, Grandma?"

Grandma says, "Because it is wintertime and some trees lose their leaves in the cold of winter. But they grow again in springtime, when the weather warms up."

Grandma clicks the button for the roll-a-door to go up, drives into the garage and then clicks it again for the roll-a-door to go down. Ivie decides to hide in the car to surprise Poppy, who doesn't know she is staying for a little holiday.

So Grandma goes inside to ask Poppy if he can get Grandma's luggage out. When Poppy opens the back door, Ivie yells out, "Surprise, Poppy!"

Poppy is so surprised and happy and gives Ivie a big kiss and cuddle. Millie, Grandma's white puppy, is excited to see Ivie too and gives her a big lick on the cheek.

This book was put together exactly how it happened with a wonderful, funny, sing-a-long, storytelling journey back to my hometown of Dubbo, NSW (from Long Jetty in NSW), through the eyes of my five-year-old granddaughter, Ivie.

The pictures were drawn and coloured in by Ivie.

What a wonderful few hours of love and laughter we had while Ivie drew some illustrations for this book herself.

Printed in the United States
By Bookmasters